THE TROJAN HORSE

Lisa Greathouse

Assistant Editor
Leslie Huber, M.A.

Senior Editor
Conni Medina, M.A.Ed.

Editorial Director
Dona Herweck Rice

Editor-in-Chief
Sharon Coan, M.S.Ed.

Editorial Manager
Gisela Lee, M.A.

Creative Director
Lee Aucoin

Illustration Manager
Timothy J. Bradley

Designer
Stephanie Reid

Cover Art and Illustration
Chad Thompson

Publisher
Rachelle Cracchiolo, M.S.Ed.

Teacher Created Materials, Inc.
5301 Oceanus Drive
Huntington Beach, CA 92649
http://www.tcmpub.com
ISBN 978-1-4333-1147-5
©2010 Teacher Created Materials, Inc.
Printed in China

The Trojan Horse
Story Summary

Long ago, a war was fought between the Greek army and the soldiers of Troy, called Trojans. The war began over a woman—Helen, queen of the Greek state of Sparta. Helen was said to be the world's most beautiful woman. Paris, the son of the king of Troy, wanted Helen for his bride. But she was married to the king of Sparta! So, Paris kidnapped Helen and brought her back to Troy with him.

Greece waged war on Troy to get Helen back. But there were huge walls around the city of Troy. After ten years of war, the Greek soldiers came up with a plan. They would build a giant wooden horse in which soldiers could hide. The Trojans would think it was a gift and would open the gates to their city. Would their trick work? Read the story to find out.

Tips for Performing
Reader's Theater

Adapted from Aaron Shepard

- Don't let your script hide your face. If you can't see the audience, your script is too high.

- Look up often when you speak. Don't just look at your script.

- Talk slowly so the audience knows what you are saying.

- Talk loudly so everyone can hear you.

- Talk with feelings. If the character is sad, let your voice be sad. If the character is surprised, let your voice be surprised.

- Stand up straight. Keep your hands and feet still.

- Remember that even when you are not talking, you are still your character.

- Narrator, be sure to give the characters enough time for their lines.

Tips for Performing
Reader's Theater *(cont.)*

- If the audience laughs, wait for them to stop before you speak again.

- If someone in the audience talks, don't pay attention.

- If someone walks into the room, don't pay attention.

- If you make a mistake, pretend it was right.

- If you drop something, try to leave it where it is until the audience is looking somewhere else.

- If a reader forgets to read his or her part, see if you can read the part instead, make something up, or just skip over it. Don't whisper to the reader!

- If a reader falls down during the performance, pretend it didn't happen.

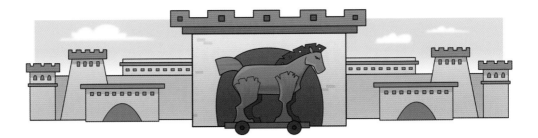

The Trojan Horse

Characters

Narrator	**Sinon** (SIGH-non)
Priam (PRY-um)	**Odysseus** (oh-DISS-ee-us)
Helen	**Laocoön** (lay-AWK-uh-wahn)

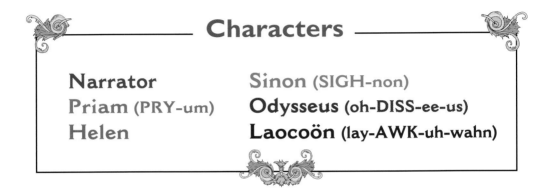

Setting

This reader's theater begins outside the walls of the city of Troy around 1200 B.C. Ten years earlier, Helen, the beautiful queen of the Greek state of Sparta, was kidnapped and brought to Troy. Greek soldiers sailed to Troy to fight its soldiers, called Trojans. The Greeks want to return Helen to Sparta. For the last ten years, the Trojans and Greeks have battled, with no winner in sight.

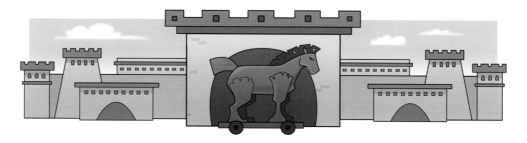

Act I

Narrator: Ten years ago, the Greek army crossed the sea to fight the Trojans. Huge walls surrounded the city of Troy. Trojan soldiers on top of the walls fired arrows and used their swords against the Greeks. On the ground, Greeks fired arrows back at the Trojans. After so many years of battle, both sides were tired and ready for the war to end. Odysseus, king of Ithaca and a Greek general, sat with his comrade, Sinon.

Odysseus: Our men are exhausted, Sinon. It has been a decade since they have seen their families. I am afraid they are ready to surrender, accept defeat, and return to Greece.

Sinon: I agree completely, Odysseus. After all these years, I wonder how many of us even remember what we are fighting for.

Odysseus: Of course, you and I remember, Sinon. Our goal is to return Queen Helen, the most magnificent woman in the world, to the king of Sparta. But we are no closer than when we got here.

Sinon: Helen has been here so long, I wonder whether she wants to be rescued. To us, she will always be Queen Helen of Sparta. By the way, I have heard the Trojans refer to her as "Helen of Troy"!

Odysseus: That may be. But still, we must try to bring her back. Those are our orders from her husband, the king.

Act 2

Narrator: Inside the great walls of the city of Troy, the people also had grown tired of the long war. Many good men had been killed in the fighting. But they refused to give up the beautiful Helen. She had become like a daughter to King Priam of Troy. Priam relied on his personal advisor, Laocoön, for advice.

Priam: Laocoön, come in, please. I need to speak with you.

Laocoön: What is it, Sire?

Priam: I need to know: When will this terrible war be over? When will life here return to normal?

8

Laocoön: Soon, Sire. For the first time, when I look at my star charts, I see an end to this terrible war coming in the near future.

Priam: Tell me more, Laocoön! What do you see? Will we be victorious over the Greeks? Will Helen remain with us always?

Laocoön: The image is blurry, Sire. But I see the Greeks going out to sea, retreating from us.

Priam: That is wonderful news, Laocoön! That must mean we will defeat the Greeks!

Laocoön: I am not confident that this is what the gods are telling me, Sire.

Priam: What do you mean? Why else would they be leaving? If they win, they will surely take over our city! That would be the vision you would see if the Greeks defeated our army.

Laocoön: Well, I also see smoke. I see their soldiers opening our gates. I also see a large horse. I can't explain these images, but they worry me, Sire.

Priam: That makes no sense, Laocoön! If you see them retreating by sea, I am sure it is because they grow tired of fighting us. They miss their families and want to return to Greece. Plus, they expect defeat!

Laocoön: Beware, Sire. As I said, my visions are blurry. You must not read more into them than you should. You should not assume that victory is ours.

Priam: Guards, get Helen for me!

Helen: You called, Sire?

Priam: Helen, thank you for coming. You look most beautiful today.

Helen: Thank you, Sire.

Narrator: Helen is bored with Priam's praise. He is the eighteenth person of the day to tell her how beautiful she is.

Helen: Why did you summon me?

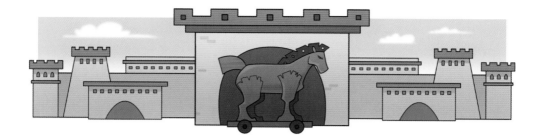

Priam: Laocoön says the war will be over soon. I need to know: If given a choice, will you stay with us here in Troy? Or, will you leave with the Greeks and go back to your husband, the king of Sparta?

Helen: I have to admit, I have grown to appreciate my life here in Troy. I am treated like royalty.

Narrator: Although, Helen is really thinking this:

Helen: Sometimes, I do dream of returning to my husband and the people of Sparta.

Priam: I am confident that we will defeat the Greeks. In fact, Laocoön's vision showed them sailing away.

Helen: I cannot imagine Odysseus leaving without victory after so many years of fighting. Odysseus is very clever. He may be planning something devious.

Priam: You think Odysseus has a plan? If he had one, why wouldn't he have used it by now? Why do you and Laocoön doubt our victory? I won't hear any of it!

Narrator: Priam storms away.

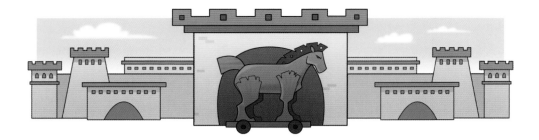

Act 3

Narrator: Outside the gates of Troy, the sun beat down. The heat made the warriors weak, and some were terribly sick. Many of them spoke of returning home. Odysseus knew he needed to do something. He sent for Sinon.

Odysseus: Sinon, I fear that we can't wait much longer. Our warriors are ready to give up. But I had a dream last night about a horse, and it gave me an idea.

Sinon: A horse? What kind of scheme did you dream up, sir?

Odysseus: I wonder if we could construct a horse out of wood. It would be large enough for some of our soldiers to hide inside.

Sinon: Sire, I believe the blazing sun has made you go mad! Even if we did build a wooden horse, and even if some of our men hid inside, why do you think the Trojans would be foolish enough to open their gates and take it inside?

Odysseus: Perhaps they wouldn't, Sinon . . . unless the Trojans thought we left the horse as a gift and sailed away. Perhaps they would even see our ships sail away.

Sinon: Ah, perhaps you're not mad after all! But how would the few men inside the horse be able to defeat the entire Trojan army?

Odysseus: Well, our ships wouldn't travel very far. If the Trojans brought the horse inside their gates, our men could sneak out during the night. Our ships would return under the cover of darkness. And the men who hid inside the horse could open the gates and let our army in without the Trojans even realizing it!

Sinon: The Trojans wouldn't even know we had taken over their city until they awoke the next morning! Sir, you are truly a genius!

Odysseus: I don't know if I'm a genius, Sinon. And of course, there is a chance my scheme won't work. But this may be our best chance of victory. Now, we must get our men to work right away. We have a horse to build!

Narrator: The next morning, Odysseus called his men together. He told them of his plan, and they all agreed it was brilliant. Odysseus assembled a team of men to cut down fifty giant pine trees in the forest. They built a wall so that the Trojans would not be able to see what they were doing. They worked day and night, and by the third day, they were finished. They had built a giant wooden horse with a hollow middle, where thirty soldiers would be able to hide. Then they put it on giant wooden wheels so that they could move it. It was perfect!

Odysseus: Sinon, I have selected the men to hide in our horse. They are the most courageous and fierce warriors that we have.

Sinon: Am I not one of them, sir? You know I would give my life for victory over the Trojans!

Odysseus: I know that, Sinon. But I have other plans for you. You will play the most important role in this ploy. When we sail away, you will stay behind. You will wear beggar's clothes and hide in the shadows. You will be the one to help convince the Trojans that our army is gone!

Sinon: Ah, so I will pretend that you left me behind. I hope my acting skills are good enough to fool them!

Odysseus: I have no doubt you will be perfect in this, the most crucial role of your life! For if you fail, I worry that the Trojans will not spare your life.

Act 4

Narrator: That night, the thirty soldiers climbed a ladder and crawled inside the horse's huge hollow belly. They pulled the trapdoor shut behind them, and the rest of the Greek soldiers wheeled the horse to Troy's gate. They packed up their things and sang as they sailed off.

Song: Sailing, Sailing

Narrator: The Greek army anchored its ships at a nearby island, where they were out of view from the Trojans. Sinon stayed behind, hiding until morning. The Greeks could hardly wait until dawn. As soon as the sun came up, King Priam called for Laocoön and Helen.

Priam: The guards report that the Greeks were seen sailing off in the early morning hours! Laocoön, your visions have come true!

Laocoön: Sire, that is wonderful news. But are you sure? What if some of them stayed behind to catch us off guard?

Priam: You're too suspicious, Laocoön. But I suppose we should have the guards patrol the grounds before we open the gates.

Helen: After all these years of fighting, I cannot believe they would leave without me!

Narrator: A short time later, a guard reported back. He told the king that the Greeks were finally gone. But he also told Priam about the giant wooden horse left at the gates. A sign on the horse said it was an offering from the Greeks to Athena, the goddess of wisdom.

Helen: That is very strange, Sire. Why would the Greeks leave a horse? You must be careful.

Priam: Helen, you are as suspicious as Laocoön! Perhaps it is simply a parting gift from the Greeks and an offering to the gods. They want the gods to see them safely home, I'm sure.

Helen: A parting gift? That does not sound like Odysseus at all.

Laocoön: Helen is right, Sire. It does seem very unusual.

Priam: But the Greeks are nowhere to be seen. Their camps are empty. We shall declare victory! I order the gates of our great city opened! We will bring the Greeks' gift inside. It will protect our city forever.

Helen: Please, Sire, beware of the Greeks' gift. I fear that this horse is nothing but a trick!

Laocoön: I must agree, Sire. Do not bring this horse inside our gates until it is fully inspected.

Poem: *Aeneid* (excerpt)

Narrator: But nobody listened to the warnings of Laocoön or Helen. The gates were opened and the horse was pulled inside the gates. Priam stood on a balcony and called out to his people.

Priam: The war is over, my good people! We have won! Our gates are finally open. Come see the gift the cowardly Greeks have left us. It is time to celebrate!

Narrator: Just then, four guards brought a prisoner to Priam. It was Sinon. His hands were bound in front of him.

Priam: Who are you? Where are the rest of your men? I demand answers, or you will be put to death!

Sinon: I have already suffered greatly. I'll tell you everything you need to know about the Greeks who have betrayed me.

Narrator: Sinon hoped that King Priam believed his act!

Priam: Why did the Greeks leave you here? Why did they leave us this horse?

Sinon: The gods advised the Greeks that they would never win this battle. The best thing they could do was to leave Athena a gift, along with a human sacrifice. They built the horse as the gift and chose me as the human sacrifice. Can you believe that? After I was such a loyal and trustworthy soldier? But I managed to escape!

Priam: See, Laocoön? It is just as I thought. The Greeks are indeed cowards! Let us bring this horse into our city and begin the celebration! Let this poor man free. He is no threat to us now.

Laocoön: Please, Sire, no . . .

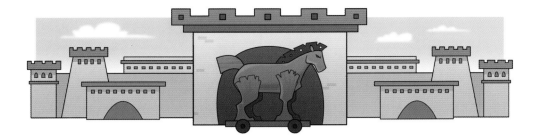

Act 5

Narrator: The people of Troy celebrated all through the day and night. The soldiers inside the horse's belly stayed silent. The Trojans pushed the wooden horse all around the city, throwing flowers and dancing around it. They ate, drank, and sang joyfully for the first time in years. They finally fell asleep, exhausted, believing that their city was safe and secure. While the Trojans slept, Sinon opened the trapdoor of the horse. He brought over a ladder so that the Greek soldiers could climb down safely. Sinon lit a fire atop the city walls so that the Greeks would see the signal and know it was time to return to Troy. The Greek army quietly docked and crept onto the beach until they got to the gates, which were still open.

Odysseus: You did it, Sinon! This is going exactly according to my plan!

Sinon: Thank you, Sire, but we have not defeated the enemy yet. I fear that one of the guards in the tower may have spotted you. I see a light on in the palace window! It is time to fight!

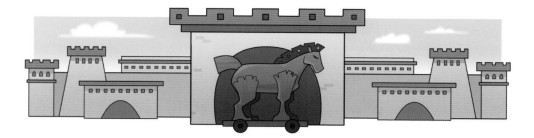

Narrator: The Greek army stormed the city, waking the Trojans with their swords. After ten years of war, the Greeks were filled with rage as they killed the Trojan soldiers and took prisoners. They captured Helen and returned her to Sparta. Before the Greeks left for home, they burned the great city of Troy to the ground. This is why the great beauty of Helen is thought of as "the face that launched a thousand ships" and began the Trojan War.

An excerpt from the *Aeneid*
by Virgil

Laocoön, followed by a numerous crowd,
Ran from the fort, and cried, from far, aloud:
"O wretched countrymen! What fury reigns?
What more than madness has possessed your brains?
Think you the Grecians from your coasts are gone?
And are Ulysses' arts no better known?
This hollow fabric either must enclose,
Within its blind recess, our secret foes;
Or it is an engine raised above the town,
To overlook the walls, and then to batter down.
Somewhat is sure designed, by fraud or force:
Trust not their presents, nor admit the horse."

This is an excerpt and translation
from the classic epic poem.

Sailing, Sailing
by Godfrey Marks

Y'heave ho! My lads, the wind blows free,
A pleasant gale is on our lee.
And soon across the ocean clear,
Our gallant bark we'll bravely steer.
But 'ere we part from freedom's shore tonight,
A song we'll sing for home and beauty bright.

Chorus:
Then here's to the sailor, and here's to the soldier, too.
Hearts will beat for him upon the waters blue.
Sailing, sailing, over the bounding main,
For many a stormy wind shall blow 'ere Jack comes home again.
Sailing, sailing, over the bounding main,
For many a stormy wind shall blow 'ere Jack comes home again!

The tide is flowing with the gale,
Y'heave ho! My lads, set every sail!
The harbor bar we soon shall clear,
Farewell once more to home so dear;
For when the tempest rages wide and far,
That home shall be the sailor's guiding star.

Chorus

This is an abridged version of the song.

Glossary

brilliant—showing great intelligence

comrade—fellow soldier; companion

confident—sure

construct—build

courageous—brave

cowardly—lacking courage

crucial—most important

decade—ten years

inspected—looked over

magnificent—most beautiful

ploy—trick

retreating—going back

sacrifice—the surrender of something for the sake of something else

scheme—plan

summon—call for

surrender—give up

suspicious—distrustful